To all the wonderful, mixed-up families
everywhere — the ones we're born into
and the ones we make along the way
A. K.

In memory of Philemon Sturges:
inspiration, mentor, and friend
B. K.

Text copyright © 2006 by Alethea Kontis
Illustrations copyright © 2006 by Bob Kolar

First edition 2006

Library of Congress Cataloging-in-Publication
Data is available.

Library of Congress Catalog Card Number 2006042310

ISBN-13: 978-0-7636-2728-7
ISBN-10: 0-7636-2728-3

10 9 8 7 6 5 4 3 2

Printed in China

This book was typeset in Futura
and New Century Schoolbook.
The illustrations were created digitally.

Candlewick Press
2067 Massachusetts Avenue
Cambridge, Massachusetts 02140

visit us at www.candlewick.com

Alpha Oops!

The Day Z Went First

Alethea Kontis   illustrated by
Bob Kolar

CANDLEWICK PRESS
CAMBRIDGE, MASSACHUSETTS

Zebra and I are SICK of this last-in-line stuff!
This time we want to go first!

IT'S OUR TURN

FAIR & EQUAL TURNS

IT'S TIME FOR CHANGE

Why not?
Let's try it!

Z is for zebra.

Y is for yarn.

X is for xylophone.

W is for whale.

P is for penguins.

P! What do you think you're doing?

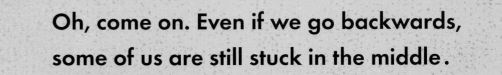

Oh, come on. Even if we go backwards, some of us are still stuck in the middle.

P is right.

AZYXWEFGHIJKLM

Here, I'll go closer to the end, just to mix it up a bit.

See what you've done?
You're making a mess!

Just you wait—this will be great!

O is for owl.

N is for night.

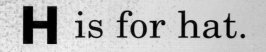

H is for hat.

H, dear, it's not our turn yet!

Just because you all want to
be different doesn't mean I do.
I happen to like being right
where I always am.

She's got a point.

S is for snake.

I is for insect.

V is for violin.

J is for jack-o'-lantern.

E is for Earth.

F is for flowers. And fairies.

A Z Y X W P O N H S I V J E

Hey, I didn't get to pick two things.

I think I should get another turn.

I don't have much
to choose from.

No more turns!

You've had your turn.

Let someone else go.

Just move it along!

T is for taxi and train.

L is for lemons and lollipops.

K is for kangaroo and kites.

C is for cat and canary in cages.

A Z Y X W P O N H S I V J E

V is for—

I said,
No more turns!

Ooh, V is for violence.

R is for raindrops and rainbow.

D is for dragon and damsel in distress.

HELP

A Z Y X W P O N H S I V J E

G is for green garden and great gorilla.

B is for big beautiful balloons blowing briskly in the breeze above a bevy of bright blue bouncing balls.

F T L K C R D U V W G B Y Z

Oops.

B is also for broom.

M is for monster.

Q is for queen.

A Z Y X W P O N H S I V J E

Is that it? Am I last?

No, A's going to be last.

Is that everyone else, though?

I can't tell, now that we're all mixed up.

Has everyone had their turn?

F T L K C R D G B M X Y O

Wait, Wait! U's been in the bathroom since
P took over. She missed the whole thing!

Do you still want me?

We're not complete without U!

Get up there, U!

U is for umbrella and unicorn.
And unique.

F T L K C R D G B M Q U Z

All right! That's everyone. We're ready for A.
A? Where are you?

I haven't seen her since H.

Jeepers, when was that?

YIKES!
You guys have
to see this!

F T L K C R D G B M Q U Z

A is for apple, accident, accordion, acorn, acrobat, airplane, alligator, ambulance, anchor, angel, angle, ant, Antarctica, archer, arrow, artichoke, artist, artwork, author, avenue, and ALPHABET.

F T L K C R D G B M Q U Z

Apology accepted.

F T L K C R D G B M Q U A

So we can all go back to normal now?

Yes. We should definitely go back to normal.

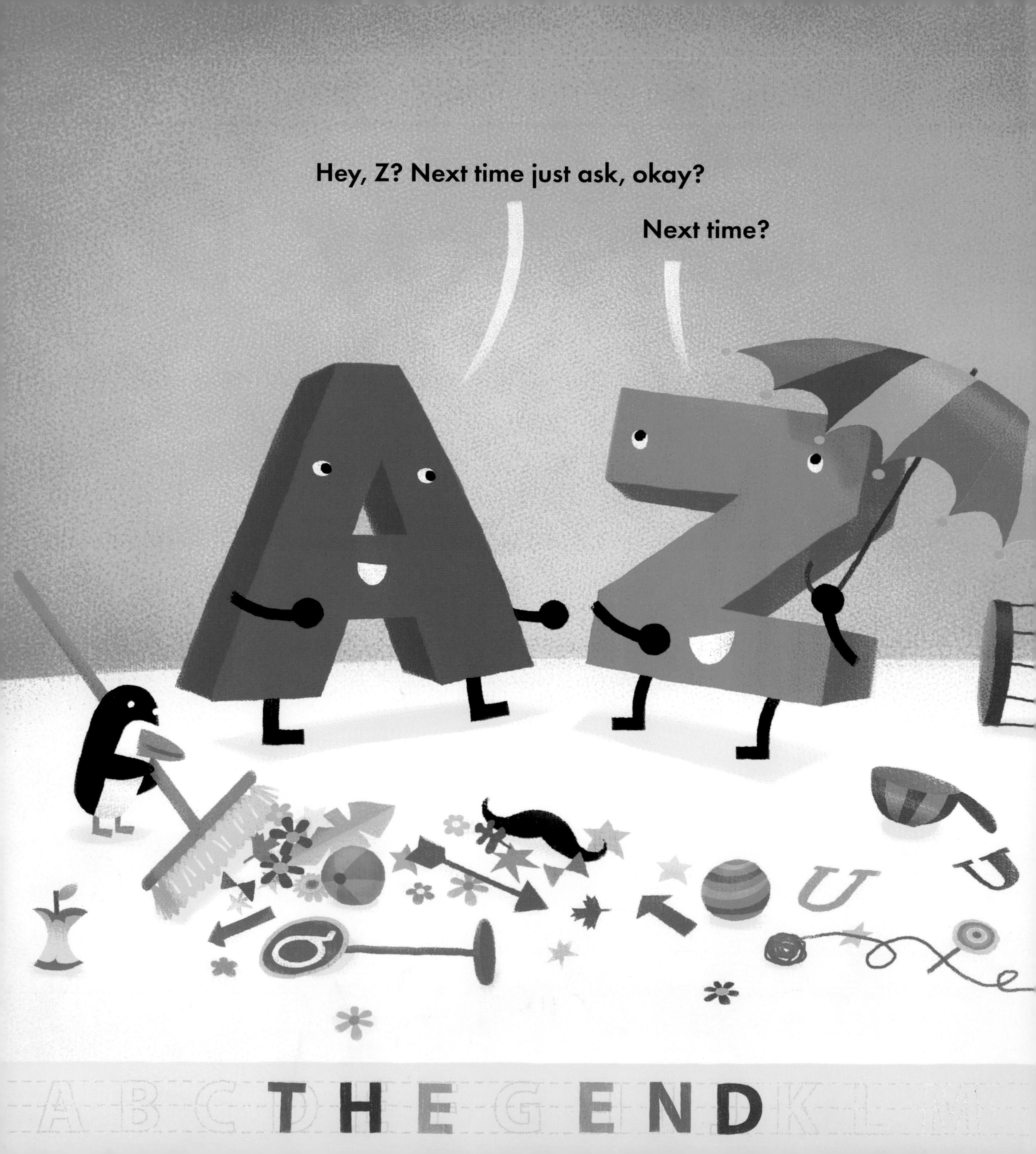
Hey, Z? Next time just ask, okay?
Next time?
THE END